THE NIGHT THAT FATHER CHRISTMAS LOST HIS WAY

Julie Carroll-Pretlove

Illustrated by Alice Roche

AuthorHouse™ UK Ltd.
500 Avebury Boulevard
Central Milton Keynes, MK9 2BE
www.authorhouse.co.uk
Phone: 08001974150

First published by AuthorHouse   11/05/2010

ISBN: 978-1-4567-0073-7

authorHOUSE®

It's Christmas Eve and Santa is due
He knows who's been good & he's searching for you
So sprinkle your Twinkles™ and tinkle your bell
To guide all his reindeer by sight, sound and smell.

For Daniel, Ben, Joe,
Will and Amy and grandchildren everywhere.

In Memory of

Don Pretlove
and
Paul Roche

One Christmas Eve, a long, long time ago, before all your mummies & daddies were even born, all the boys and girls were snuggled down in their beds, with their teddies, trying very hard to fall asleep. They knew that Father Christmas was on his way to bring them their presents. Now, I'm sure that everyone knows that if you <u>aren't</u> asleep Father Christmas doesn't come but sometimes, because after all Christmas Eve is the most exciting night of the year, it's really hard to go to sleep. Do you think so? Well it was just like that in the bedroom of Daniel in the story that I am going to tell you. Daniel was a little boy who lived in a house just like yours and he was just the same age as you are now when this story happened.

It was very dark on this Christmas Eve and the moon was hidden behind a huge cloud so that there wasn't any light shining anywhere apart from the orange glow from the street lamps all along the road. Daniel had been lying in bed for what he thought had been ages but he could not get to sleep.

He was tossing and turning, trying to find a comfortable spot in the bed but his mind would not stop thinking of the surprises that he hoped he would soon be getting. He knew that he wasn't supposed to be awake, but he just couldn't sleep! Just then Daniel heard footsteps coming along the street; they stopped at the corner near his house and suddenly he heard a group of voices directly under his window, singing, #Silent Night, Holy Night# .Dan crept quietly out of bed and rushed over to the window to look outside.

He grew even more excited when he saw that a white blizzard of snow had covered his entire garden. He then saw where the singing was coming from, a group of Carol Singers all wrapped up warm with bobble hats and scarves had congregated outside his gate and were singing from the carol sheets which they held in their gloved hands. Dan had never seen them before and enjoyed watching and listening to them so much that when it was time for them to walk away to the next house he had not realised how cold he was, standing at the window and out of his snugly warm bed. Just looking at the snow made him feel icy cold but at the same time the excitement of know-ing that Father Christmas would soon be here made him feel warm inside as well. The snow lay thick on the ground and even as he watched, the footprints of
the carol singers were being completely covered by the freshly laid blanket of snow flakes which were falling like white feathers from the sky. Daniel loved watching the snow as it softly and quietly fell, to hide all the objects in the garden – the fence which was usually dirty and broken now looked beautiful and clean with its new fresh coat of snow white paint and the bare leafless trees which had seemed so sad with their bare stick branches now suddenly seemed happy and bright dressed in their snow white sleeves. He jumped back into his bed and shivered a long, cold shiver, bent his knees and rubbed his feet up and down the bed quickly to warm a spot.

Earlier that evening his Mum had told him while they were having tea that Father Christmas had already set off on his long journey from the North Pole and would already have started delivering some of his toys to the children who lived far away.

Just thinking about this gave Dan a warm feeling in his tummy. He told himself that he must go to sleep. He closed his eyes and hummed his favourite carol to himself, "Away in a Manger, No crib for a bed........" but no, he still wasn't asleep and he found his mind wandering again to where Father Christmas was and how far away from his house.

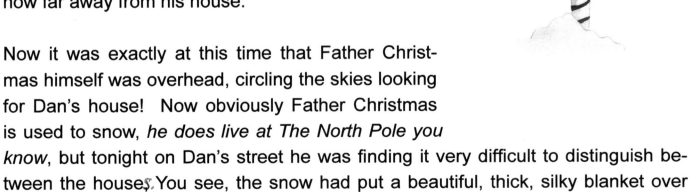

Now it was exactly at this time that Father Christmas himself was overhead, circling the skies looking for Dan's house! Now obviously Father Christmas is used to snow, *he does live at The North Pole you know*, but tonight on Dan's street he was finding it very difficult to distinguish between the houses. You see, the snow had put a beautiful, thick, silky blanket over everything in sight: the roofs, the paths, the fences, the gates, *everything!*

As Father Christmas looked down at the street below he didn't know what to do with himself, he couldn't just guess which house was Dan's because he might end up giving his present to someone else! Then what would happen on Christmas morning?... everyone opening other people's presents, no-one getting what they had asked for! Christmas could be ruined for everyone.

Then it came to him, Father Christmas knew how he could find Dan's house; he could get his magical reindeer to help! This was a complex dilemma and Father Christmas knew there was only one reindeer clever enough to figure out a solution, Blitzen, the smartest of all his reindeer! "Blitzen!" shouted Father Christmas "I can't find little Daniel's house and he has been such a good boy this year we can't let him down! What can we do?"

Now as we all know, usually Rudolph with his nose so bright would have easily guided Santa's sleigh but unfortunately he was poorly in bed and unable to help on this particular Christmas Eve.

Blitzen shouted to all his reindeer brothers and asked if they had an idea. "Come on boys", said Blitzen, "Santa needs our help." They all thought for a while and then they came up with a bright idea...

"Santa, why don't we circle over the houses and you can shout for Daniel to wake up and show us where he is."

"Well," said Santa, "I don't usually let all my lovely children see me but that is a good idea and I think it's the only way I will be able to deliver all my presents tonight. Good boy Blitzen."

So that is exactly what they did. All the reindeer flew down lower and lower to just above the chimney pots of the houses.

Then, Father Christmas shouted with all his mighty voice:

"Ho Ho Ho, Daniel can you hear me? This is Father Christmas calling Daniel. Where are you Daniel? Where are you? I can't find you. Help my   reindeer find you Daniel....". He said this over and over again as the reindeer circled the skies searching for Daniel's house.

Now, back in his room Daniel was in bed but still not asleep, luckily, and as he was lying, still thinking of Father Christmas, he suddenly heard a very strange sound, one which he had never heard before. It started as a quiet tinkle and grew gradually louder and louder until he recognised it as the sound of sleigh bells. What could it be? Daniel asked himself. Then, he   heard the distant sound of someone shouting and when he listened very hard he heard that it was his name. He jumped out of bed and dashed to the window to see what or who it was. AND THEN,,,, he saw it... a brilliant, brightly lit sleigh with all the coloured sparkling lights you could ever imagine and in front of it 8 beautiful reindeer all pulling with all of their might.

Then as Daniel's eyes searched the spectacular sight he saw who was sitting in the sleigh.....FATHER CHRISTMAS himself, his hands cupped to his mouth, calling Daniel's name. Daniel couldn't believe his eyes or ears when he heard that Father Christmas was calling him and asking for <u>his </u>help.

What should he do? ...What could he do that would help Father

Christmas find him?... Do you have any ideas?

Well, I'll tell you what Daniel thought of. He quickly put on his dressing gown and slippers and crept down to the kitchen. There, he reached up into the cupboard and pulled down a box of porridge oats. (How clever of Daniel to know that a reindeer's favourite food is porridge oats!)

So he poured out a handful of the oats into a dish so that the reindeer would be able to smell the food and it would guide them to his house... but then he thought. The snow was very thick outside and although they would be able to smell the food, they still might not be able to see exactly where the house was. What else could he do?

Well just then Daniel remembered a present Santa had left him last year... it was an art set with some magic sparkling glitter which Daniel had loved so much that he had saved some. NOW was just the right time to use it. He poured the magic sparkle into the dish of oats. He crept to the front door and carefully opened it, letting in a huge gust of cold air.

Daniel did not care about the cold...

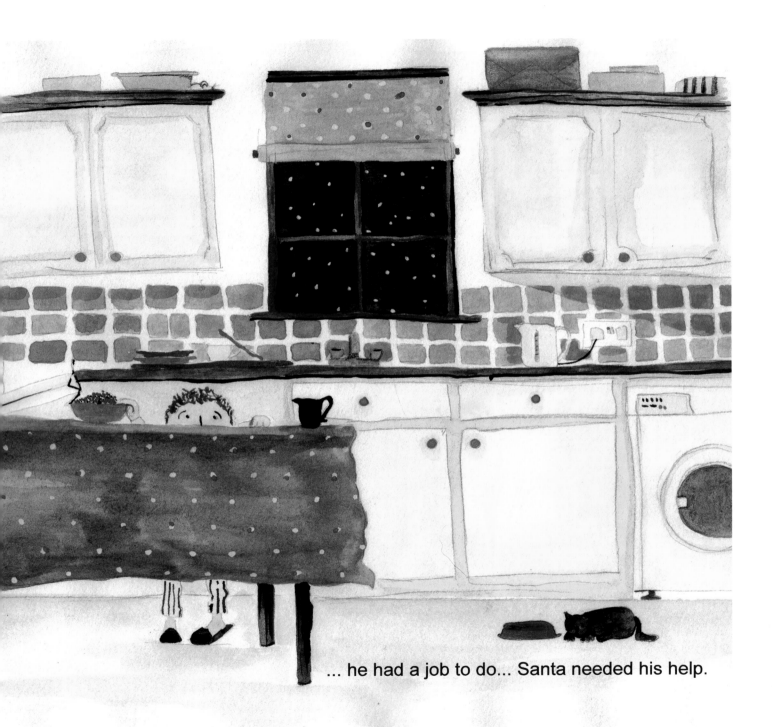

... he had a job to do... Santa needed his help.

Carefully carrying his dish of magic reindeer food, he walked down the snow covered path in his front garden, leaving a trail of deep footprints behind him.

When he reached his gate, he looked up to see if the sleigh with the reindeer and Santa were still close by. Sure enough, there, right above his head was the magic sight. He could hear Santa still calling him but neither Santa nor the reindeer could see him yet.

He quickly but carefully sprinkled the reindeer food onto the ground in front of him and walking back to his front door laid a trail which the reindeer could follow. Then Daniel took off the belt from his dressing gown which had small metal tassles at the end and waved them in the sky to make a noise like a bell.

Meanwhile, up in the sky, Santa and all the reindeer were looking very hard to see anything down below which they could recognise which would help them find their way again.

Suddenly, Blitzen's nose started twitching, and then almost at the same time all the reindeer did the same. Dasher and Dancer, Prancer as well as Vixen, Comet and Cupid, Donner and Blitzen all could smell the food and at the same time see the magic sparkle of the glitter. Within seconds, they knew where they were and swiftly glided down, bringing Santa and his sleigh full of presents right down to Daniel's front garden.

Well you can imagine how happy Daniel was and how relieved and grateful Santa was. After big hugs all round, Father Christmas told Daniel to pop back to bed and go straight to sleep. He promised that in the morning when he came downstairs that he would be very surprised. Then in seconds he was gone and all Daniel could hear from his bed was the distant sound of sleigh bells as he faded into the distance with the cheerful Ho Ho Ho of Santa as he moved on to the next little girl and boy.

The next morning when Daniel woke, he ran downstairs and of course he found a huge pile of lovely presents but the most special gift he found under the tree was a special letter from Father Christmas and his reindeer thanking him for his very clever trail of reindeer food... and guess what?.. another massive bag of magic glitter!! That was the best Christmas for Daniel!!!

Now that is the end of our story apart from one thing...

This happened a long, long time ago and now Daniel is a very old gentleman with children and grandchildren of his own but do you know that to this day, every single Christmas Eve, Daniel makes up a special bag of reindeer food and just before he goes to bed, he goes outside and sprinkles a trail for the reindeer to follow... just in case!